One

This is a true story about three JACK RUSSELLS, beginning with Becky, her daughter Cyndy, and grandson Toby.

One Saturday afternoon in the month of November 1974, our son Ian was given a bedraggled pup by his girlfriend. The pup was eight weeks old. At first we thought this pup was brought home just to show us, but in fact it was for keeps.

As much as we loved dogs in the past, this pup was not welcome because within minutes of being let loose in the room it did a big job - oily and really smelly! That was enough. Ian was promptly told to take it back from where it came.

Ian assured us that if he returned the pup there was a possibility that it would be put to sleep because it was in very poor health and by no means a cuddly pup. Ian was serious in what he said, so we decided to keep her until a suitable home could be found for her.

We named her Becky, and she remained with us: try as we did, no one wanted her. Eventually, the unwanted became the wanted in our home. While the family were at work, my aged mother took her into the garden as often as possible to do her bits and pieces, but during the night she continued to mess in the house. I had to do something about this problem. The answer was to clean out the coal bunker and keep her in there during the night.

To make it comfortable inside the bunker, I placed a wooden box containing a foam mat and plenty of straw to keep her warm. Of course, she never took readily to her nightly abode and had to be enticed into the bunker with a bowl of milk which she soon came to know as her "night-cap".

Once locked up in the bunker she never yelped or barked until let out in the morning, when she really got excited, rushing indoors upstairs and downstairs then into the garden where she would wet and do her job. In fact, the coal bunker was generally clean, so much so that it was not long before she was accepted in the house not only by day, but by night as well; in other words Becky had become a member of the family, loved by all, though very fussy about being handled by strangers.

From being a bedraggled, thin and ugly-looking pup she had developed into a beautiful little dog, but still keeping her puppy-like looks. Naturally, many people, especially children wanted to handle or touch her. Of course, knowing her nature

To, John & Margaret
Hope you find this book
of interest.

With best wishes,
Mike. Harrison.

AND NOW THERE IS ONE

Michael G Harrison

Harrison
22nd Sept 97

MINERVA PRESS

LONDON

MONTREUX   LOS ANGELES   SYDNEY

ISBN 1 86106 485 3

First Published 1997 by
MINERVA PRESS
195 Knightsbridge
London SW7 1RE

Printed in Great Britain for Minerva Press

AND NOW THERE IS ONE

we immediately warned them not to touch her because of her tendency to nip. However, times arose when it was too late and her needle-sharp teeth drew blood from a hand or fingers. Of the many such incidents there are two incidents which readily come to mind.

The first was on a visit to Bristol. My nephew Tony Rigby and I walked into the Cloak and Dagger Public House. Becky was with me. A problem arose when I saw a notice: "DOGS NOT ALLOWED". I decided to ignore the notice and picked Becky up and hid her inside my coat, then went to the far corner of the room and sat down while Tony walked over to the bar to get the drinks. No sooner had I sat down when an elderly lady came along and sat beside me. She saw Becky's head protruding out of my jacket.

"You have a puppy hidden under your jacket," she said.

"So I have," I replied, thinking to myself of the trouble to follow. But to my relief came these words:

"Don't worry, I'm a dog lover, and have a Jack Russell myself!"

A friendly atmosphere established, we discussed the behaviour of Jack Russells in general until Tony had his say by condemning dogs with a remark that they were treated better than humans! The remark was scorned at by the lady who then leaned towards me and asked ever so politely, "May I hold the puppy?"

"I'd rather you not. She might nip you!" I replied quite seriously.

She replied very positively saying, "I cannot explain why, but for some unknown reason there is such a bond between dogs and myself that they won't bite me!"

Having said that she immediately held her hand out to stroke Becky who showed signs of unfriendliness by lowering her ears and lifting her lips to show her teeth, but the lady never withdrew her hand, as a result of which it had to happen. Yes, she gave a sharp growl and in a flash nipped the lady's fingers!

"You see," I told the lady, "I did warn you!"

"Most extraordinary! I have never been bitten before. I guess there's always the first time." Having said that, embarrassed no doubt, she gulped her drink and hastily left, surprisingly without a threat.

On another occasion, some days later while visiting Bath, I waited outside a store while my wife Sheila and her sister Wynn went inside to browse around. It was a bitterly cold morning so I picked Becky up and held her in my arms. A woman walked by looking eagerly at Becky then stopped and came back a few paces to have a really good look at her.

"What a pretty face she has. Where did you get her from? How old is she? What's her name?"

The questions answered, I knew what the lady would say next. Sure enough the request came in an appealing manner. "Please let me give her a little cuddle. She's gorgeous!" I had to disappoint the lady by politely telling her that Becky bit strangers if they tried to handle her.

"Not if you talk to a dog affectionately, then offer your hand with the palm facing downwards and the fingers bent inwards. Perhaps I should tell you that I'm a dog trainer and breeder." She was certainly very convincing. For that matter, so was Becky because she showed her teeth as soon as her hand came near and within seconds, before a tender word was spoken, Becky drew blood from her knuckles!

Gradually Becky's temperament improved. She became very obedient, and wasn't ever-ready to bite, though as far as children were concerned she was untrustworthy. On the other hand she adored babies and appeared to get quite upset if they cried. Her immediate reaction was to lick their feet, hands and face. Something Natasha still remembers.

I took her out regularly every morning at about 6 o'clock, before leaving for work. Of course, she always greeted me on my return, except one evening when she was absent when I opened the door. In spite of all my whistling and calling for her she failed to appear at my feet or jump up to be cuddled. Naturally I got quite worried, but then consoled myself with the fact that sometimes my son Ian or Mick got home before me and took her to the park.

Half an hour or so elapsed without Becky's return so I drove to the park, the recreation ground and Wimbledon Common, the usual places where Becky was taken. To all my enquiries I got negative answers. Becky or any of the children had not been seen. Now the time had come to really worry.

All sorts of things went through my mind. She had access to the rear garden at all times through a cat-flap, therefore I didn't rule out the possibility of her chasing a cat and managing to climb over the garden fence and into a network of alleyways.

I telephoned the local police enquiring as to whether a Jack Russell answering to the name of Becky had been found. The answer was no. I got the same reply from Battersea Dogs' Home. As a last resort I went to my allotment where I often took her ratting. Once again a disappointment.

I was now convinced she had been stolen. It was easy enough for someone to climb over the fence and offer her a bone – something she would beg for under any circumstances – for her to become an easy capture. We could not rest that evening; the search continued in the neighbourhood until late at night. We were heartbroken. It was like losing a member of the family. After all, she had become one.

Awakening earlier than usual, I opened both front and rear doors and whistled in the hope that if Becky was somewhere near the house she would come running in. No such response. I wrote a letter to the local *Guardian* newspaper to advertise a reward for Becky's return.

Having washed and dressed I was all set to leave for work when I remembered I had to take a pair of pliers with me. As I opened the door to the storage space below the stairs, out shot Becky, leaping up and down full of excitement, then raced upstairs to greet Sheila and the boys, and within seconds came charging down the stairs to see if there was any dinner in her bowl!

I remember having gone into the storage space under the stairs, and no doubt Becky must have followed me and got locked in when I shut the door. If only she had barked or whinged the ordeal would have been over much sooner. Perhaps she imagined she was playing a game of hide and seek, but forgot about time!

Becky's favourite, other than a bone or chocolates, was a ride in the car. And what's more, she had to sit in front, between the passenger and driver's seat, where for her comfort a small pillow was placed. Yes, we made a great fuss about

her, but unfortunately we made a big mistake by giving her the pillow between the front seats. This created a problem because for some unknown reason she disliked the use of the handbrake. The driver used it at his or her own risk. And what do you think that risk was? A bite on the hand was a certainty, albeit just a friendly one!

One day I forgot to tell a relative about Becky's reaction to the use of the handbrake. He borrowed my car to take members of the family, including Becky, to Richmond Park. Well, John got to Tibbett's Corner then took the A3. He was forced to stop at the traffic lights at the road linking Roehampton. Naturally, when he stopped he applied the handbrake. Becky immediately bit his hand!

"You horrible bitch," shouted John.

"You skinhead... roadhog... nasty man!" came a reply from a girl sitting in a convertible BMW car in the overtaking lane, awaiting the traffic lights to change to green!

Almost every evening when indoors, Becky was taught new tricks. It is said that dogs are colour blind, but there is always the exception to the rule. Becky was no ordinary dog, she knew the difference between red, blue, yellow, white, etc., because we lined up various coloured balls and told her to bring so-and-so colour. Generally she picked up and handed you the right coloured ball!

She enjoyed her training classes as much as we did. Her intelligence increased to the extent that she learned to understand the spelling of common words such as walk, car, park, rats, cats, bed and many more, even "no biting", though at times she ignored those words, perhaps intentionally! A few words mentioned caused absolute confusion in the house or elsewhere. These words were cats, rats and squirrels. If she heard any of these words she would rush out into the garden in a frenzy, barking madly to see off the intruder. On the other hand you'd ask her the question "Who's that?" This would bring a different response. She would dash to the front door barking louder than ever. In fact, if anyone knocked at the door or rang the bell, they met a hostile reception. If you opened the door with a key, she knew it was a member of the house, so there was no barking whatsoever. To test her intelligence I once gave the house key to a friend to come in at a given time. As soon as he got to the door and tried to open it he met with a series of barks, an indication that someone other than a member of the household was attempting to enter the house!

Jim Watts and I drove down to visit his family at Bighton, a small village near Alton, Hampshire. In addition, we were also expected to shoot wood-pigeon which were plundering a farmer's wheat crop. We obliged, after which he made a further request, an unusual one, that being to get rid of hundreds of rats taking shelter amongst bales of straw in a storage room alongside his barn.

I was not prepared to believe the farmer's story, nor Jim's, that when rats collect in such large numbers they can actually move a bale of straw! Well, the proof was to come later. We commenced lifting out bale after bale of straw, during which every now and then rats leapt out from beneath to be met with a walloping by sticks. The more bales removed, the more rats took cover under the remaining bales until there remained just two. These two bales lying adjacent to each other were actually being moved by the vast number of rats sheltering beneath them!

The time for action had arrived, we stood with sticks at the ready while two farm workers lifted the bales off the floor. There was absolute bedlam. Rats ran everywhere, up trousers, across the body, on to the head, from where they jumped to any escape route they could find. The massacre over, we rubbed our own wounds, inflicted by the frenzied use of sticks in a restricted space. Some of the rats killed were enormous, almost the size of a guinea pig.

Of course, a number of rats were seen to escape and take shelter amongst rusty old farm machinery which lay in a heap near the barn. What has all this business got to do with Becky, one may ask. Well, she was there, but only as an onlooker, tied to a large wheel from where she yelped madly, no doubt seeing the occasional rat go past out of her reach.

Her real excitement was about to commence; my only worry was in case she encountered one of those very big rats. As luck would have it she didn't. Lead and collar removed, she bolted straight for a spot overgrown with weeds, old buckets, parts of machinery and corrugated sheeting. In no time at all she was dashing about after rats, snapping them up, followed by a few quick jerks for an outright kill, repeating the act one after another, her tongue hanging out and almost touching the ground. She certainly had a field day, living up to her breed's reputation as 'ratters' – another name for Jack Russells. Whatever you call them they have character of their own; they are intelligent and always lively. No wonder you see them on TV adverts – other than those promoting dog foods!

Often, after rainy weather Becky entered the house, her paws coated with slush. Naturally, we told her she had dirty paws and went about wiping her paws clean. Eventually she took an immense dislike to the words "dirty paws". It wasn't long before we dare not use the term dirty paws without Becky getting very angry – firstly showing her teeth, followed almost immediately with an attempt to bite the hand, even though it be the hand that fed her!

Becky was fully matured, over a year and a half old when I began to take her out shooting. She was a source of interest, chasing anything that moved, from horses to rats, from pheasants to chickens. She became a nuisance rather than an asset as far as my shooting trips were concerned. Finally I had no choice other than to leave her at home when I went out shooting.

One morning, accompanied by a good friend, Jim Watts, we went to visit Mr Spencer at his Manor on the Norbury Estate, Mickleham. Not expecting to spend much time there I took Becky along for an outing, and what an outing it turned out to be! A disaster from the word go. This is what happened.

Getting out of the car (without applying the handbrake!) we walked along the edge of the woods towards the mansion. Becky picked up a scent and away she ran into the bushes, up a little hillock, where she rushed about in circles. No way would she listen to my whistles and shouts to come back so I hurried across to put her on a lead. I was too late to stop her entering a rabbit warren. In fact, there were plenty of these scattered down the slope. Near to where Becky entered, rabbits bolted out only to re-enter the network of warrens again. I knew Becky was after them, but she never surfaced despite calls and whistles down these holes.

We spent well over an hour in search of her, hoping she would emerge from somewhere. As a last resort Jim borrowed a spade from the gardener and we commenced digging where I'd seen Becky disappear. It was a very tiring job. We took turns to dig along the tunnel which was large enough for Becky to move along in a crouched position. To turn around was impossible so she had to go forward. This is where the danger lay. The tunnel narrowed, a junction appeared, she could now have taken any direction. We had to face facts: Becky could get stuck underground forever. It became a real nightmare. How could I explain her loss to the family?

Digging at the best of times is very hard work, more so when meeting up with chalky areas such as we were now faced with. Hours had passed and it was my time for a rest. I sat with my elbows resting on my knees, my hands covering my face. I could see visions of Becky stuck helplessly in a dark maze of an underground wilderness, best known to rabbits. The short rest over, I removed my hands which covered my eyes and looked down the slope. I imagined I saw a movement, something whitish amongst shrubs about twenty yards below.

I immediately ran down to have a look. I couldn't believe my eyes when I saw Becky lying exhausted at the mouth of a warren!

Her normal pure white smooth hair was dirty and ruffled, and there was traces of blood on her face, chest and forepaws, no doubt the result of catching, and perhaps killing a rabbit. It didn't take her long to fully recover from her experience. She was soon jumping all over me with excitement at being united once again.

Becky was about three years old when we thought the time was right for her to have pups. Of course, Becky, being Becky, was fussy about the Jack Russell we approved of as a mate for her. She refused to allow two other such dogs to come near her, with threats to bite. However, I met a Mr and Mrs Wheatland at a pub who had two lovely Jack Russells. I told them about Becky's behaviour. They gave me their address, a farm just outside Dorking and assured me that if I brought Becky there next day she would find a dog to her liking. I took her as arranged and she met The Duke of Dorking, their champion dog. Becky immediately fancied him; they ran about the farm house enjoying themselves.

With Becky's Dorking affair over, my wife suggested we visit her sister Wynn and her husband John Bateman, at Whitchurch, a suburb of Bristol. Becky was a bit of a problem because of having to share the house with a rather vicious tom-cat. They had met earlier when Becky was a pup, even then their short meeting was far from amicable. However, on arrival, measures had been taken to ensure they did not confront each other.

All went well. We spent much of the time away from the house taking Becky with us. Wynn had a ten-year-old son Richard, who was by no means an angel; in fact, like most boys of his age he was quite a rascal, ever ready to promote a fight between Becky and the cat if he got the chance. Therefore a close watch was kept on his movements whenever such a possibility could arise.

John had made arrangements with Tony Rigby to help him put up an extension to his garden shed. Well, another pair of hands was more than welcome with my presence. Sunday breakfast over, work commenced. John climbed the ladder, the plastic sheets were handed to him which he placed on a wooden framework, and commenced to screw them down.

As often happens when a novice tries to build something, an error, or errors occur. A supporting pillar needed adjustment which was possible provided it was held firmly from below. Tony and I got a good grip on this pillar and gave John the all clear to go ahead with the job he had in mind.

I believe that Richard must have been watching the work going on because at the precise moment when Tony and I took hold of the pillar, he must have let the pet rabbit out of its hutch, then gone indoors to allow Becky out into the back garden where she knew a rabbit lived.

Becky emerged into the garden like a rocket, yelping as she picked up the scent, traced the rabbit and chase commenced. At this moment our natural reaction was to save the rabbit. Forgetting that John was dependent on our firm hold of the pillar, we immediately ran forward to save the rabbit, which we did; but there was a terrific crash behind us. Yes, John was left to plunge down into a heap of wreckage and complain about his injury to his right leg which would make it difficult for him to walk to the pub for a drink before lunch. We told him not to worry. Four wheels is better than one or two legs!

The commotion over, dog, cat, rabbit and Richard kept apart, and the job we set out to do was successfully completed in spite of John's repeated complaints of the injury he got because of Becky. To emphasise his injury he straightaway massaged his right leg, surely an act to gain sympathy!

After a period of relaxation we drove to a lake where Becky was given the freedom of the countryside. Typical of her, she jumped out and ran, perhaps picking up the scent of fox or rabbit. Richard followed at full speed with not a hope in hell of catching up – nevertheless, they did return together.

Stopping on our way home at a pub where even the likes of Becky was welcome, we consumed a few drinks when Tony, at an appropriate moment, asked John, "By the way, how is the pain in your leg?"

"Still bad," he replied, rubbing his left leg!

Becky was soon to become a mother. As the time neared, she became very restless looking for a place where she could have her pups. To help her find a suitable spot, I took the box out of the coal bunker in which she herself had spent time as a pup and placed it in our room. She entered the box several times, eventually settling down on the night of 23rd April, 1976, to produce a handful of pups comprising four bitches, the lot of them looking like her and the father... white and tan.

By morning Becky had become a demon. Becoming a mother had changed her from bad to worse. The pups had become untouchable except to me. Later, however, she allowed my wife Sheila to handle them, but on no account would she allow Ian or Mick to enter the room to see, let alone touch them.

The only way others could see or handle the pups was firstly to get Becky out of the room. To do that the quick way was to loudly say the word 'cats'! Becky would instantly jump out of the box and rush downstairs, barking as she went, to search the garden where the odd cat was occasionally seen. In her absence the pups were handled without any fear of Becky having a go at the unwelcome visitors to the room. However, to open the door to the room with Becky waiting to enter was risky, because she knew the children or visitors were with the pups. It was quite funny really, when the door was opened to see Becky rush in and the others leap over her to get out of the room as quick as possible!

The pleasure and fun the pups gave us for over two months was soon to end when the painful partings commenced. The first to go was Kim, the spitting image of Becky, followed at short intervals by Bella, Bunty and Cyndy. Poor Becky, lost without all her pups, roamed about the house in search of them, every now and then uttering a whine, especially when she frequently visited the locked coal bunker where I'd placed the box after all her pups had found new homes.

Cyndy, a timid, but extremely affectionate pup went to a lovely home. They were recently retired people who had all the time in the world to share their happiness with Cyndy. They lived in New Malden, not far from Wimbledon Park, so we often visited them, taking Becky with us. The mother-and-daughter relationship was as strong as ever. Together they played about as they did in our house. About six months later, the couple went on holiday and asked us if we would look after Cyndy. Naturally we did, and the bond between Becky and Cyndy once again grew very strong, which was bad in a way

because after two weeks or so Cyndy went back, leaving Becky to fret all over again.

Cyndy was a year old when she was brought back to us because of the gentleman suffering a stroke and being admitted to hospital.

According to the lady, she was out shopping when her husband suffered the stroke and fell down the stairs. On her return she found him lying at the bottom of the stairs breathing very heavily, with Cyndy licking his face and hands. Unfortunately, he never recovered from the stroke and we were asked to keep her because his wife would be moving to a flat where pets were not permitted. So Cyndy was back with her mother Becky, the queen of Jack Russells!

The two of them, as usual, got on very well together though Becky made it clear that she was boss in the house and in the car. Yes, Becky stood no nonsense about sharing the bean-bag, lying across in front of the calor gas heater so that Cyndy had no option other than to find a place behind or at the side of her. As far as the car was concerned, well, Cyndy was definitely not welcome in the front seat. She tried several times to sneak in but always met a hot reception. Eventually, Cyndy came to know her place: the back seat!

The two of them looked quite similar in size and colour, but there was a world of difference by way of nature. Becky, as you know by now, was snappy, whereas, in contrast, Cyndy wouldn't say boo to a goose. She was an absolute angel. Children loved her and she loved everyone. Unlike her famous, or I should say infamous mother, she never ever nipped anyone. No wonder she was so popular, especially with children. I walked the two regularly in Durnsford Recreation Ground; in doing so I passed numerous school kids, some stopping to ask "Which is Becky ?" Once that was established, they immediately made a fuss about Cyndy, picking her up, cuddling her, and above all, sharing a piece of chocolate with her, much to the envy of Becky! Aware of this discrimination, I always carried a few dog-chocolates to give Becky to equalise matters.

One morning in autumn, the lake in Wimbledon Park was carpeted with leaves. Ducks and coots swam amongst the leaves while those that sat on the embankment flew into the water when they saw Becky and Cyndy approaching. On previous occasions the ducks remained quite far out in the water so that the dogs took little notice of them, but because of the leaves or reasons best known to the ducks they swam about close by. Becky stood and watched them, but Cyndy must have thought they were on land and took a spring across at the nearest ones. The shock must have been terrible to land in water and almost sink! Anyway, she turned around and frantically swam towards me but couldn't get out of the water because of not being able to climb the embankment. I lay down, stretched out and hauled her up.

I saw the funny side of Cyndy's unexpected swim, and thought of the proverb which suited the incident: "Fools rush in where angels fail to tread." Actually, Cyndy was quite silly compared with Becky considering that she did another foolish thing some months later when the same lake froze over. Once again I was walking the dogs in the park and when we approached the lake near the boathouse, mallard ducks, coots and Canada geese flew down off the footpath on to the ice. Becky stood at the edge, barking at the wildfowl which were skidding about quite amusingly. Cyndy was in the bushes in search of rats, then came to join us. She too barked at the nearby mallards which got a bit frightened, and skidded about; some fell over, others managed to take off. This behaviour was new to Cyndy who must have thought there was a chance to catch one. She leapt forward and to my horror went through the ice. She tried hard to get out from the hole, swimming desperately in freezing water. Fortunately for her she was about five feet away and the water shallow enough for me to smash through and rescue her. At the best of times she felt the cold, but in these freezing conditions and soaking wet she looked as though she was about to die. I can only describe her

shivering to that of a flag in a strong wind. Carrying her to the car, an act Becky always felt jealous about, I got home, rubbed her well in a towel then put her in front of the heater, much to the annoyance of Becky, who in this case of emergency was given the elbow. Cyndy lapped up the heat, recovered from the jaws of death, and then knew she had been given Becky's place right in front of the heater. The favouritism over, Becky was allowed to be boss again.

We went to visit friends, the Loughran's at Langley Vale, Epsom. They weren't in, so we took the dogs up the hill to the woods near the Epsom Race Course. Becky and Cyndy soon picked up a scent, presumably of a rabbit, fox or squirrel, and disappeared out of sight. Barking commenced in two different places a short distance apart. The closer of the two was Cyndy, which I knew because she had the louder bark. Heading towards her, I expected to see her barking at a squirrel up a tree, often as the saying goes "barking up the wrong tree!"

To my surprise, she was barking very angrily at something underneath the trunk of a fallen tree. It took some time before I got her to leave this spot, then catching up with Becky we took

another chance to meet our friends, but they were still out so we returned home.

As usual Becky was the first out as soon as the car door was opened followed closely by Cyndy. But she just sat there, looking awfully sorry for herself. We noticed her mouth was terribly swollen and so were her eyes. Really, her whole face looked swollen. I took her immediately to the vet, Ian Smith at Tooting, and jumped the queue to produce Cyndy's ugly face before him. He asked me a few questions as to where she had been and how long her face had been so swollen. At first he said it must be a bee or wasp sting, then doing a further test he diagnosed the awful swelling to be caused by snake-bite, probably an adder's. She was kept overnight in the vet's clinic for treatment and observation.

I collected her next afternoon. There was only a little swelling to be seen on her upper lip, otherwise she was quite happy. At home she was missed by Becky who made a great fuss on her return by licking her all over the face; then they chased each other all over the rooms enjoying themselves.

It was Christmas morning. Becky and Cyndy sat watching the unwrapping of presents taken from underneath the colourful Christmas tree. They got their presents as well: a rubber ring and a bone each. The excitement over, I took them for their morning walk to the recreation ground but the gates were closed, a notice read 'OPENING TIME 9 AM'. Rather than go home I walked them along the narrow road running between a line of small workshops and the recreation ground fencing.

Bins had been left outside many of these workshops, some without lids and full to the top with Christmas party leftovers. One of these bins aroused a keen interest to both the dogs. They kept jumping up and trying to get into the bin. I knew straightaway that there must be a rat in the bin so I tilted it over. Becky, followed by Cyndy, got in, their paws working faster and faster to empty out the rubbish comprising beer-cans, plastic cups, paper and food containers. Suddenly they both barked. There was panic in the bin until a huge rat, almost the size of a half-grown rabbit jumped out and ran towards the hedges.

Within seconds Becky had it in her mouth, shaking it from side to side, so fast that Cyndy couldn't get a look in until all of a sudden Becky uttered a painful yelp and dropped the rat, but the rat had its teeth into Becky's cheek. Cyndy seized this chance to put her teeth into the rat and grabbed it away from Becky. Between them they tore the rat to shreds.

I noticed that Becky was bleeding badly from the mouth. In fact, when I took a close look, the blood was oozing out of her cheek and coming into her mouth. The wound was deep and about an inch and a half long which must have been caused when Cyndy grabbed and pulled the rat away from Becky. At that moment the rat had its teeth into Becky's cheek, so really, Cyndy helped to make the wound bigger, but not of course on purpose. I took Becky to the vet; fortunately he lived on the premises, and though closed for business on Christmas Day, he was very good to attend to Becky, giving her another Christmas present: nothing more, nothing less than seven stitches in her cheek!

Becky showed no signs of any ill-effects due to the injury caused by the rat. The wound healed, the stitches were removed and Becky was once again ready to join the fun and games she loved so much. But not for long. New Year's morning when let out of the car she was waiting for Cyndy when a car went by and knocked her over. The driver slowed down after the collision and must have seen me pick her up because he then sped away. As much as I wanted to get after the driver, my first concern was to attend to poor Becky who was bleeding from the mouth and ear. In fact, she looked as if she was dying, gasping for breath as she lay on her side in my arms.

Sheila hurriedly put her on a blanket and covered her up and we drove off to the vet. He was on holiday, but had a notice on the surgery door giving the name and address of another vet who could be seen in an emergency. We took Becky there. He examined and X-rayed her, then assured us that she should be OK, but he would have to keep her in the clinic for at least two days. Naturally, we were very upset during her absence. However, the phone rang for us to come and collect Becky. We took Cyndy along to greet her mother. They were so happy, especially Becky, to be sitting in the car and heading home, once again to be united with the family.

Cyndy was six years old when we decided that she should have pups to be fathered by Sam, a very good-looking black-and-white Jack Russell, well-known in the Kingston area, and claiming to be related to the Jack Russells belonging to the famous Jimmy Tarbuck!

Well, it wasn't long before Cyndy began to put on weight. She was definitely going to have pups. It was quite amusing to see her try and keep up with Becky when it came to a chase after a squirrel or rabbit. Usually Cyndy raced ahead of Becky, but now she was way behind, surely unable to believe that Becky had started to run faster than her. No matter how hard Cyndy tried she got slower and slower until the time came when she could hardly walk, let alone run. And when she walked, she waddled like a duck! Yes, the time had come to have her pups.

She roamed about the house looking for a spot: our bedroom, under the bed, appeared to be her choice, but not for long.

She'd be off again looking for another place, yet still in our bedroom. I suddenly thought of something, the box in which she was born! It was stored in the coal bunker, so I got it out, cleaned and lined it with a strip of an old blanket and placed the box in a corner of our room.

Strangely enough, she accepted the box without any fuss at all, as if she'd remembered that this box was the place of her birth. She settled down in the box for the big event at about 6 p.m. Sheila kept a close watch on her for a few hours. She got out of the box, came downstairs, did a wee in the garden then found she couldn't climb back up the stairs. Picking her up gently, I carried her up the stairs to the bedroom where she sniffed about before getting into the box. Once again she settled down quite comfortably. We checked on her every now and then to see if she was giving birth.

Sheila knew that Cyndy was having labour pains, and it would not be long before she would have her pups. Sheila kept vigil for hours, listening, watching, without a pup being born. At about 3 a.m. there was a lot of shuffling in the box. Sheila put the bedroom light on to see what was happening. Cyndy was in serious trouble. A complication had set in. A pup was stuck in the uterus, and try as hard as she could, she could not deliver the pup.

I phoned Ian Smith, the vet. No answer from him so I rang another vet, namely Mr Kidd, at 5.30 a.m. and told him about Cyndy's problem. He told me to bring her down immediately to his clinic on Leopold Road. This done, he examined Cyndy and said "I'm afraid I've got to do a Caesarean operation immediately, but you and your wife will have to assist me because the nurse will take time before she gets here."

Sheila declined to face the operation, but I had no option other than to help the vet, who shaved Cyndy's stomach and cut her open after giving her anaesthetic. Removing the pup from the uterus he handed it to me saying "Don't worry about this pup. It's dead. That's how it is." Three more pups were handed to me at short intervals. To me they all looked as if they were dead. However, I did what I was told, that being to massage them really well, one at a time in rotation. The nurse arrived and straight away helped the vet in the stitching-up business.

No matter how hard I tried to get the pups to start breathing they still looked dead to me. Then between the nurse and myself the pups got quicker massaging, as a result of which one pup began to breathe and utter very soft squeaks. This was the second of the three pups handed to me by the vet. Shortly afterwards, the third one did the same, but the first one removed still would not respond to the massaging even though done by the nurse and the vet himself. I was very upset because this one looked ever so much like Becky, and we couldn't get him to breathe or utter any form of noise.

It was almost time to put him with the other dead one when a miracle occurred. There was movement in his tiny paws followed by the faintest of a squeak. I had him in the palm of my left hand, bent over and started to gently blow warm air on to him. We were all amazed as to how soon he started to breathe, quite freely, and what's more his squeaks turned into gentle little yelps to match those of his brother and sister. When we left the clinic at 6 a.m., Cyndy was still very dazed, just about recovering from the anaesthetic; the three pups, however, were full of movement and airing their lungs.

Back home, we put the pups into the box, keeping Cyndy lying comfortably close by until she fully recovered from her ordeal. Meanwhile, Becky had come to check on Cyndy's long absence and finding her lying flat on her side, looking very sorry for herself and smelling of medication, she showed a lot of concern by licking Cyndy all over the face. Then she heard the pups, anxiously looked into the box, stepped in and took charge of the pups as if they belonged to her!

Trouble arose when Cyndy stood up in a daze, took a few paces, sniffed about, then I suppose came to her senses and realised she had pups. She went straight to the box to face a growl from Becky. Cyndy was always timid and docile, but motherhood had now changed her. She growled back most angrily, ready for a fight. I immediately picked Becky out of the basket. That was the last thing we wanted, a fight between the two of them, especially as Cyndy had just come out after having a serious operation. Anyway, we kept them apart, not allowing either of them to be with the pups because Becky was unable to foster mother them, and Cyndy, due to the operation, was not allowed to feed them for at least two days. So all we had to do was bottle-feed them until Cyndy was well enough to let the pups help themselves to mother's milk.

Though we kept Becky away from the pups by keeping the bedroom door closed, she sat for hours just waiting for a chance to get to the pups. To give Cyndy a chance to leave the room without Becky getting in, all that had to be said was cats! Both of them would be down the stairs and in the garden, barking their heads off. Becky being by far the more clever of the two, she'd pretend that she'd found the cat, and as soon as Cyndy was attracted to the spot, Becky was gone like "Lamplighter Dick" to be with the pups!

Within a week, Cyndy had taken complete charge of her pups, feeding and cleaning them, at times even allowing Becky to share the pups with her. Eventually, it was lovely to see such a great relationship develop after the pups came along between Cyndy and Becky. I believe the pups, named Toby, Bella and Scooter, never knew who their mother was because they got on so happily as family. Having said that, Becky, though loved, was respected and feared by the pups. A gentle nip taught them to behave themselves if they stepped out of line.

Once again the unhappy time approached to part with the pups. Tears were shed when Bella, very much like her mother in looks and nature, went away with Mrs Everett, a wonderful old lady who absolutely adored Jack Russells. So Bella was going to live in the lap of luxury in the Wimbledon Park area. Scooter, the bully amongst the litter, loveable all the same perhaps because he was such a rascal, had a black patch on his face making it easy to identify him from his brother and sister. He also went to a good home not too far from us, but later enjoyed the countryside of Wiltshire with Laura and Paul Bartlett. Toby, my pride and joy, was the last to leave home. He too was just around the corner at Southfields, so really it was a pleasure to meet often in the park and watch the five of them play happily together like they did in old times.

One evening the woman who owned Toby telephoned me to ask if I could come over to see her. I did so to be greeted firstly by Toby, then came the bad news. She and her husband had separated. Neither of them could now look after Toby, therefore she asked me to take Toby away and find a home for him. What a terrible thing to happen! For no fault of his, he had to go. Just as in the case with Cyndy, he was back with us, fortunately accepting the position as a junior in the house, though he was much bigger than his mother and grandmother.

Sheila's sister Wynn and her husband spent a short holiday with us. They took a liking to Toby and asked if they could have him. We agreed so off Toby went to a house beside a farm on the outskirts of Bristol. I believe he was ever so happy there, enjoying his walks in the countryside, chasing rabbits and also doing a good job in the farm where he got rid of quite a few rats.

A year or so later, Wynn telephoned to say that Toby had bitten her teenage son Richard on the face, quite a nasty bite at that. She was worried about him being bitten again and was going to get rid of him, unless of course we wanted him back. We couldn't believe that Toby would bite anyone, especially a member of the household. He had such a wonderful nature. Anyway, we drove to Bristol to pick him up, taking Becky and Cyndy with us.

On arrival at the house Toby was all over us, then went rushing off with Cyndy and Becky as if to show them around the fields where the rabbits were to be found. However, when leaving, he wasn't keen to get into our car until he saw Cyndy sit up in the back seat. He jumped in, not realising the trip he was about to take would be a farewell to Bristol.

Back home he recognised familiar places; how to get out into the garden through the cat-flap; where the bean-bag was; where he ate and drank; and above all where the rubber balls were kept. When it came to walks, be it in the recreation ground, park or the woods on Wimbledon Common, he knew exactly where to go.

One thing I noticed about Toby on his return back to Wimbledon was his hatred towards motorcyclists. He just could not stand the noise of a motorcycle or anyone getting off or on one. I was told that Richard rode one himself, and in addition had many friends who came up to visit him on motorcycles, revving the engines, at times purposely annoying him. Of course, their dress was different to ordinary people he met everywhere and the helmets worn by motorcyclists made them look strange. I do believe he bit Richard because he must have teased him after removing his helmet or just tried to stroke him. I had all three of them on a lead when a motorcyclist stopped to ask me directions. Toby immediately tried to attack him, something he'd never done before, so this bad habit started in Bristol when he first came in contact with motorcyclists.

I was having an informal chat with Chief Inspector Doug MacNicoll who was at Wimbledon Police Station. During the course of the conversation I raised the question of the Neighbourhood Watch Scheme being introduced to the Wimbledon park area where in fact I lived. He gave me the guidelines to start the ball rolling. Well, I approached many of the residents, a meeting was held and the scheme was introduced.

It was a very hot Saturday afternoon. Indoors was like an oven, the answer to which was to open both the front and back doors to allow what breeze there was to circulate through the rooms. I was aware of the fact that it was an open invite for a burglar. On the other hand I also knew that the dogs would not welcome a stranger into the house, so we had peace of mind enough to relax and watch TV in cooler conditions.

Chief Inspector MacNicoll was carrying out a routine patrol of the area when he noticed my residence on Stuart Road with wide open doors, inviting crime. Naturally, this would give him a wonderful opportunity to enter the house and have the pleasure of criticising my negligence in keeping out burglars.

The metal gate needed lubrication, but I intentionally left it as it was because when it was opened it squeaked. This was a signal for the dogs to check as to who was entering the premises.

Well, Chief Inspector MacNicoll was lost for the words he had in mind for me when he faced the combined attack by three Jack Russells, all of them barking in a frenzy. Utterly astonished at the reception he encountered, he just about managed to shut the gate in time to avoid the sharp teeth of Jack Russells.

A Jack Russell is not to be seen in the line-up of dogs at the famous Crufts Dog Show because they have not been recognised as a pedigree breed. It's a great pity considering they are attractive, intelligent and clean, and often seen on TV adverts, not to mention as a trade mark for the old-fashioned HMV gramophone and amplifier, showing a Jack Russell listening in.

To overcome this discrimination, The Jack Russell Club UK was formed. They hold their own championships and various other functions, generally at country fairs, so they have become quite popular and well-attended.

One of many Jack Russell Meetings took place at Bramley, near Guildford. The highlights at this fair were Jack Russell races across rather rough ground. A dummy rabbit was pulled along quite fast by means of a simple pulley system operated by a cycle wheel. About ten dogs took part in each race. They ran along a corridor formed by spectators, owners and supporters, the noise of some sixty or more Jack Russells yelping all together was deafening before, during and after each race. These dogs are excitable at the best of times. This was hilarious.

Our three took part in separate races. Toby was in the first group to go and got boxed in so wasn't amongst the winners. Becky was next. She got a flying start and was surely amongst the winners, but ran on and on until out of sight. I don't think she saw the dummy disappear! I found her eventually still looking for the rabbit. Cyndy ran in my absence. I believe she was a slow starter and just followed the pack.

However, there were other attractions such as the best dog, bitch, etc., being judged. I entered Becky and Cyndy in a group 'Mother and Daughter'. They were very good and obedient, and walked beside me without pulling. They were awarded second prize. Should have been first: unfortunately Becky's tail had been judged to be docked too short. Not her fault!

I entered Toby in a class he was suitable for, above the height limit. I stood with him amongst others awaiting the judge's orders to start walking the dogs. Toby, for some reason, started to pull away, to sniff the leg of the person who stood next to me. Then to my embarrassment and an outburst of laughter from spectators, Toby cocked his leg up and piddled on that chap's slacks! After this display of misbehaviour, how could he be judged a prize-winner?

Our house is close to the flight path of aircraft heading for Heathrow airport. Though aircraft fly over reasonably quietly, some are more noisy than others, not that it really bothered us, but Toby made it known that he either liked or disliked Concorde by rushing out into the garden and barking. His sense of hearing in those days was extremely good, for that matter so was his eyesight. The peace and quiet of the house would suddenly be broken by Toby uttering his loud bark and continuing to do so in the garden. Almost inevitably, within about fifteen seconds Concorde would be seen or heard on its way to land at the airport.

When we went on holiday, while the boys still lived at home, it wasn't too bad for the dogs though we believed they did fret for a few days. However, after the boys left home we had to ask friends to look after them while on holiday. On one occasion it was for a period of five weeks. A friend, Rita Woodford, took them away to her house at Tunbridge Wells. Her house was close to a wood and also a large farm so they enjoyed themselves to say the least: it was a holiday for the dogs as well.

The next holiday we planned, the dogs had to stay at home to be looked after by a friend, namely Charles Olney, who lived two doors away. Somehow, Becky knew that we were going on holiday. I suppose she saw the suitcases being packed. At times, if the lid to a suitcase was not shut, she would be found inside, sitting or lying quite comfortably to make sure she was not left behind!

During another long holiday, a month to be exact, Pearl Smith, a lovely lady living on our street, agreed to do what Charles had done the year before. Holidays came and went, and not only Becky, but Cyndy and Toby also began sensing our departures, so all packing was done in a closed room, and just before departing from the house, all three of them would be given a juicy bone so that they would be busy chewing bones while we left the house unseen.

Returning from one such holiday, we were given the usual happy reception by all except Becky, who walked away sulking, as if to say, 'Why did you bother to come back?' Another time, we were going away for just a week or so. As usual, before leaving the house, they were offered a bone each. Becky refused to take hers because she was intelligent. She had come to know that bones, if offered before their dinner time, which was about 5 p.m., were suspicious, probably because we were about to leave the house to go on holiday. Yes, she was almost human. At times like this, she'd be miserable – watching Cyndy and Toby relish the bones given to them, whereas, instead of her mouth watering to get her teeth into a bone, her heart must have been overflowing with tears.

I had been suffering with angina, a heart complaint which went from bad to worse until I had to have a bypass operation to save my life. The operation was carried out successfully by Dr Pepper at St George's Hospital, Tooting. I was in hospital for about ten days, visited by Sheila and my sons regularly. I was told that the dogs were fretting, and sometimes refused to eat their dinner, most of all Becky, who must have sensed I was in hospital by getting the smell of medicines off Sheila after she had visited me. After all, she must have remembered the times she was in a clinic getting treated with medicines.

When I came home the dogs got so excited that I got worried. The reason – no other than all three of them jumping at me to be picked up. I could hardly stand, let alone pick any one of them up. Of course, they weren't to know I'd been sawn down the chest to the stomach, and cut from the groin to the ankle to remove a vein. This meant I was in great pain and very weak to lift anything.

Since my return from hospital the dogs couldn't understand the change of their routine as far as walks and drives were concerned. I couldn't take them for their long walks through the woods or drive them to various parts of Wimbledon Common. At the usual times in the mornings and evenings, they had a habit of arriving at my feet, sitting down and staring at me as if to say 'Come along, it's time to go for a walk!' Those days were over, for the present at least, though Sheila took them at various times for quick walks to the recreation ground.

I rested a lot on my bed or on the settee, and Becky often jumped up to be by my side. I was advised by the doctor to let plenty of air get to the wounds. Of course, it didn't take long before Becky sniffed out and saw the scars of the operation. It is natural for animals to lick a wound to heal it. Becky really became a nuisance. She was determined to lick my wounds better. Eventually, all three of them started to do the same. I suppose Becky had passed the word around that I had injuries!

After about three weeks I started taking them out to the top of the road and back, a very short distance indeed, and that too at a snail's pace, their leads tied to my belt. Any attempt to pull me along was soon stopped by threatening them with my walking stick, a new introduction to their lifestyle.

As the saying goes, time is a great healer. The walks got longer, eventually as far as the park, where I rested while they made up for lost time. Some days however, I didn't feel too good, taking them as far as the recreation ground, letting them off their leads to play around for long periods, while I rested on the benches from where I kept an eye on them. One morning they went mad by continually leaping up the trunk of a tree, at the same time barking excitedly. I was at the other end of the ground, but try as hard as I did to call them back they just took no notice at all. Their behaviour forced me to walk across to them, and as expected, there was a squirrel looking down at them just out of their reach. The squirrel was being defiant because it knew the dogs could not jump any higher, however hard they tried. Naturally, the dogs were getting angrier and angrier because no squirrel had ever been so defiant and unafraid of them before. To make matters worse, when I put the dogs on their leads and walked away from the tree, this unusual squirrel followed behind the dogs annoying them all the more!

Some days later the same thing happened again. This time there were quite a lot of school kids with grown-ups. They were very amused with what they saw, some boys pleading with me to let the dogs off the leads when the squirrel followed right across the recreation ground. Another morning this squirrel followed the dogs all the way home, crossing Durnsford Road at the zebra crossing! One gentleman suggested I get in touch with the BBC or ITV to film this strange behaviour of a squirrel with a pack of Jack Russells. Whatever happened to this squirrel is anyone's guess. I never saw it again.

I had fully recovered from the operation and was due to fulfil a promise to visit my brothers and sisters in Lincolnshire. It would also be nice to test out my new Astra hatchback on a long-distance trip. With our change of car from a saloon to a hatchback, Becky lost her privileged place near the handbrake to join the others at the back. Nonetheless, she took up the centre with Cyndy and Toby on either side.

The car packed, we set off at first light in spite of which it took almost an hour to get out of London. Somehow, none of the dogs liked long-distance travel. Time is what mattered. Anything over fifteen minutes or so would bring moans and groans from Toby to be let out. Things worsened if we didn't stop. He commenced to bark, becoming louder and louder, and he knew he was out of reach to get a smack. We stopped at a lay-by for a few minutes, let them roam about in the bushes, then drove on. Once again he started his barking to let us know it was time to stop. We had some refreshments with us so I kept an eye out for a suitable lay-by.

This stop turned out to be a real headache. No sooner had they jumped out of the car when Becky, as usual, picked up a scent and ran across a ploughed field, followed by Cyndy and Toby. All of a sudden a hare jumped up in front of Becky. The yelping and the chase commenced until they disappeared over a hillock and out of sight! That's all I wanted to make sure they never came on holiday with us again.

I followed in the direction as fast as I could until I reached the crest of the hillock, from where, out in the distance I could see three white objects, undoubtedly the dogs. They were quite far apart, then after a while got together and followed each other in no frantic hurry until they saw me. They knew I was angry, keeping well out of reach, running like hell to get to the car so that they could jump in and save their skins. Not so lucky, they sat at the back of the car unable to jump in, resembling the three proverbial monkeys, "Hear no evil, see no evil, speak no evil."

Arriving at my sister Clare's house, the dogs checked out the garden and the rooms. They had their dinner, and later settled down for the night on their bean-bag in the closed-in porch.

I was dressing when suddenly all three dogs started barking at the same time, followed by the noise of footsteps running over the pebbled path which led to the porch. The paper boy delivered the newspaper every morning quite happily until he almost died of fright when he was putting the papers through the letter box into the porch and the dogs leapt at him, their paws striking against the glass!

The next morning there was more trouble. This time it was the postman and the milkman who were forced to retreat from the porch, the milkman actually dropping and breaking a bottle when he turned round and ran! My sister said "I think you all should cut short your holiday with me and move on, otherwise I'll get no papers, mail or milk!" Of course, it was only a joke. The deliveries continued with amusement rather than anger.

Packing our suitcase and other bits and pieces didn't worry Becky at all. She knew that she was away from home; all her things, the dinner bowl, the rubber ring and all the balls, including the bean-bag, were also being packed into the car so she knew she wouldn't be left behind. As for Cyndy and Toby, well, they just depended on Becky's intelligence and followed her.

All set the dogs waited at the back of the car to be let in. The farewell over I drove off to cover the next fifty-odd miles to Sibsey, near Boston, to spend some time with my brother Ainsworth and his wife Evelyn. As usual, Toby started getting restless. I stopped after half an hour's driving at the entrance to a dirt track leading to a farm. A bad choice because all three of them set off for the farmhouse, causing absolute chaos amongst the chickens and ducks, and then sniffed out rats in an old shed. It took me some time before I was able to get them back to the car. Fortunately the farmer was out, otherwise the dogs could have been at risk of being shot at. What a terrible tragedy that would have been.

Arriving at Sibsey, a lovely little village, we were made very comfortable, including the dogs who were accommodated in the conservatory attached to the rear of the bungalow which was a great relief, because all deliveries such as newspapers, milk and letters would be trouble-free, not like what happened at my sister's place.

My brother and I took the dogs for a walk along a public footpath, a dyke on one side and acres upon acres of cabbage fields on the other. The dogs as usual picked up the scent of something and went down the bank of this deep and narrow dyke. Taking little or no notice of them we walked on discussing various matters both home and abroad.

Every now and again Toby would overtake us then force his way into the bushes etc. growing in the dyke. Not seeing the other two, I looked back quite often and became concerned. We waited a long time before commencing a search for them. The dyke, as I've mentioned before, was overgrown with bushes and the narrow banks were very steep indeed. However, I struggled down and walked along the shallow water, slush and bog. It was hard going. Then I heard the noise of splashing feet and found Cyndy absolutely exhausted trying to climb the steep bank out of the murky water. I helped her up on to the footpath. There was still no trace of Becky.

Both Ainsworth and myself walked in opposite directions along the dyke in search of her. There was no doubt about it that she was somewhere in this dreadful narrow wilderness of reeds, bushes, bog and patches of water. After rescuing Cyndy, I was filthy so it wouldn't make much difference to get into the dyke again and search for Becky. It was a nasty business walking through what is best described as a punishment course.

Becky was now over eleven years old, and this must have been very hard going for her. What I had foreseen all along did happen. I found her stuck in thick slush with only her head, neck and the top of her back visible. She was in a terrible state, pathetic to say the least. When I lifted her out of the muck I found I could not climb out of the dyke with her! Eventually, a place was found from where I pushed her up the bank, then got out myself. These dykes can be real death-traps for animals with short legs who are old, like Becky.

It wasn't long before Becky had commenced to struggle to keep up with the others and found she could not jump into the car, try as hard as she did, sometimes several times. She depended entirely on me to lift her in, though she managed to jump out OK. In spite of age becoming more and more of a handicap, Becky was still boss, keeping the best place in the car, the bean-bag and in front of the calor gas heater. She commanded seniority and respect to the very end.

The time eventually came when she could hardly walk; nevertheless, she accompanied the others, though I carried her most of the time. Fortunately she was light so I was able to carry her for quite a distance through the woods which she thoroughly enjoyed, especially when the others chased a squirrel up a tree. Whenever this happened she struggled to get out of my arms to join the chase. All that she could do was sit and bark when I put her down under the tree around which the other two would rush about just as she had done not so long ago.

She remained very much alert, never lost her good looks, but became entirely dependent on being carried if taken for a walk. One morning in the woods on Wimbledon Common I was carrying her while Cyndy and Toby were going mad about not one squirrel, but about four or five of them up a small oak tree. Hearing the noise an old lady appeared, and seeing me carrying Becky asked, "What's happened to her?" I told her that she was very old and couldn't walk. "How nice of you to do that. I wish I could find someone to carry me!"

The inevitable time had come to end her days of agony. She was now in the last stages of liver failure. She couldn't eat or drink, nor even walk a few steps. It was pathetic to see her in this condition. The family had passed the verdict that we should let her leave us forever, yet no one would take her to the vet to be put down.

I couldn't face work the day I made up my mind to take her to the vet. That afternoon I carried her through all her favourite haunts, especially the woods of Wimbledon Common. She was still alert to know that Cyndy and Toby were barking up trees, but made no effort to free herself from my arms as she had so often done before. I became very sad, my vision was blurred with tears, knowing that shortly Becky would never see these places again. Yes, places she loved as a pup, and later worked as a team with her daughter and grandson, teaching them how to chase rabbits and squirrels. Soon, we would be left with her two presents to us: Cyndy and Toby.

Driving to the vet with the three of them was bad enough. Returning home with two was even worse. Becky had given us fourteen years of affection and entertainment and naturally would be missed by everyone. At the very start, as we got home Cyndy and Toby would not go indoors. They sat looking up at the car waiting for Becky to be let down. For some weeks they still continued to sit and wait for Becky to be lifted out and placed on the kerb. Eventually, they realised she had parted for good and the two of them returned to normal, though for some time afterwards, if we mentioned the name Becky they would immediately show interest, and at times go looking for her.

In and outdoors, life continued as normal for the two of them. If anything, Toby was a little better off because, while Cyndy wasn't bothered about playing with rubber rings and balls, Toby now had a whole lot more – Becky's plus his own. He enjoyed playing with a ball when taken to the recreation ground or the open spaces elsewhere. Cyndy would occasionally chase after a ball to get to it before Toby, but would never retrieve it. On the other hand when they were taken to any woods, especially on Wimbledon Common, they didn't want to know about playing with a ball. All that mattered then were squirrels and rabbits.

I took them as often as possible to woodlands, and as the weeks, months and a few years went by, Cyndy began to slow down just as her mother did. In due course when she tried to chase a squirrel or rabbit, I could see that the spirit was willing but the flesh was weak, very weak. She couldn't keep up with Toby. I gave her every encouragement to keep going, often using the word cats or squirrel, even if there were none around, just to make her do a bit of running.

Then came the time when she wanted to be carried, just as I'd done with Becky. Perhaps she remembered me doing it.

Finally I had to give in and start carrying her exactly as I'd done with Becky. It wasn't long before I had to take her to the vet to do what all dog owners dread. Anyway the vet gave her a new lease of life for two days, then another injection which kept her alive for another day. It was hopeless: she was old and suffering with the same complaint as her mother. Next day she was to be put to sleep.

I carried her through the woods before taking her to the vet. She watched Toby, still fit as a fiddle, chase squirrels and try climbing trees after them. It was her last view of these lovely places. And once again when we got home, Toby waited and waited and waited, but like his gran, his mother Cyndy never ever came out of the back of the car again. Yes, she had gone to join her mother in the great unknown, leaving Toby to look after the house and family that had given them such a wonderful home.

Toby was now very lonely. He went from room to room, barked in the garden hoping that Cyndy would join him, something she had always done. As for the car rides, well for months he waited for her to join him but eventually went off alone, perhaps hoping to meet up with her on a squirrel or rabbit chase. Anyway, he appeared to be happy enough, taking more and more of a liking to tennis balls, and above all, Becky's large blue rubber ring which at one time all three of them would tug at from different directions, the tug-of-war getting noisy with awful growls, sometimes ending up with a fight. He often brought this ring to me so that it would be like old times, except that now it would be just the two of us. He was remarkably strong. Any wonder why Becky and Cyndy got angry when he usually pulled them along.

His interest in balls continued, the larger the better. He had to get his teeth into them, until they burst. This became costly because when he saw kids having a game with a rubber football he invariably burst it and got me into trouble, so all that I could do was to ask the price of the ball and pay up! As for tennis balls, if there was one to be found, he would find it more often by smell than by sight. I say this because on several occasions I would find him missing in the park or recreation ground. I'd soon find him in the hedges watching a tennis ball out of his reach! And, unless this ball was handed to him, he would come back again and again until you did so!

Friends, Ken and Eileen Cumine, living at Winchester were determined Sheila and I attend their son's 21st Birthday party. We accepted provided Toby, our dog, was also invited! He was, and enjoyed himself as everyone else did. On our way home we took the M3 Motorway. Toby moaned, groaned and barked, but we could not stop to let him out on a motorway. However, just before getting home we let him out on the recreation ground where I threw a ball to exercise him. He went hell for leather after the ball, then suddenly curled up in agony, unable to walk. Compared with Becky and Cyndy he was a heavyweight, nevertheless, I managed to carry him the short distance to the car.

Back home he continued to limp badly. I thought by morning he'd be OK but, that wasn't the case. The limp had worsened so I took him to the vet, a place he hated, just as most dogs do. Having said that, Becky was the only dog I knew who was quite happy to visit a vet. Anyway, Toby had to be carried into the clinic because he refused to walk in. The result of the examination indicated that he had sprained his leg very badly and that he should be given plenty of rest. Easier said than done! However, after a few weeks of being taken out on a lead he was as energetic as ever, though ever since he developed a slight limp; perhaps it had become a habit.

Friends from Canada, Peter and Daphne Perkins, stayed with us for a week before going on to Hong Kong. They insisted that on their return to Canada, we fly over and spend a holiday with them. The offer was very tempting, especially with its promise to spend time in the Rocky Mountains. We told them we would come if we could find someone to look after Toby. Once again the energetic and always helpful Pearl

Smith agreed to take care of Toby who got on very well with her.

On our return from a wonderful holiday, we found Toby in tiptop form. Pearl told us that he was no problem at all and she enjoyed the time spent with him. Only one day she got a bit worried because Toby sat below a shelf refusing to move from there. A biscuit was offered. Oh yes, he ate that quick enough then sat like a statue again in the same place. At last, Pearl noticed a tennis ball lying in a bowl on the shelf which she picked up and showed to Toby. I believe he begged for it, thereafter was as happy as ever playing with it. Like a metal detector, Toby is a tennis ball detector!

By the age of ten, Toby was overweight. I had to put him on a diet which made little or no difference other than making him miserable. He went in search of tit bits even to the extent that he started pinching the bread thrown out for the birds. The birds didn't like this, neither did I, so the birds were fed on a stand out of his reach. He got the message. No extras for him anywhere.

I often took him through the alleyways before entering the recreation ground. On one such walk through an alleyway he met up with a cat which actually attacked him. It was strange that Toby was taken by surprise and beaten up by a cat. After the quick, short fight, I noticed Toby had a smear of blood under his left eyelid. I had another look at it when we came home. It was just a little scratch. Nothing to worry about.

Some weeks later I noticed that his eyesight wasn't as keen as it used to be at ground level or above. He never used to miss any movement, which gave me cause for concern. I took him to the vet. It was bad news. In addition to an eye infection, he had cataracts. The vet prescribed eye drops which I treated him with regularly without much good. Gradually, his eyesight went from bad to worse and by the time he was eleven years old he only had partial vision.

To help him along with his walks, which had now become quite slow, I jingled bells to let him know that I was nearby. Whether he could see me or not, he followed the noise of the bells I kept on a key ring. If I stopped jingling the bells, Toby would get confused and sit down. This reaction of his convinced me that he was now blind. Even at home if any item of furniture was moved elsewhere, Toby would get lost or bump into things. This behaviour of his convinced us that he was totally blind.

Every morning I take him by car to the park from where he walks along the path to the edge of the wood and back. He has come to know the land marks such as pillars, benches and certain trees. I was out rather late one morning when a blind person with a guide dog, accompanied by a lady, stopped and spoke with me, enquiring as to how old Toby was, and as to why I jingled the bells. I told them that he was blind and I had taught him to follow me by jingling the bells. The blind person was absolutely delighted to know I was caring for a blind dog by saying "Ironical. Here I am being led by a Golden Labrador, and you are leading a blind Jack Russell. How wonderful. You have made my day." We meet occasionally. The blind greets the blind.

Most of his life now is spent sleeping on the large bean-bag once shared by Becky and Cyndy. It's placed beside the master radiator so when the central heating is put on, he really laps up the warmth. Some mornings when it's freezing I open the door to take him out in the car to the park. He walks out, feels the freezing conditions and walks straight in again to the comfort of the bean-bag! Can't blame him. After all he must think to himself, "It's pointless exposing myself to such cold when I can't see anything, neither can I run about to warm up." He did get excited one day, and showed it by picking up the scent of a squirrel. The run ended abruptly when he crashed into the first tree that came in his path. Since then he has never ever attempted to change gear again.

It is nearing two years since Toby has lost his sight. To add to his discomfort, he is fast becoming deaf, but thank God his sense of smell, which has always been good, is in fact getting much better! He smells his way out to the garden, follows his tracks from room to room, has favourite spots where he lies down, other than the bean-bag. He knows exactly where Sheila and I sit and comes at regular times to get a Good Boy chocolate from each of us.

All in all, we do as much as we can under the circumstances to keep Toby content. Dogs wag their tails to show happiness, but poor old Toby, and he is old, has never been seen to wag his tail since becoming blind. Mind you, he has only a stump for a tail, so it's not easy to wag.

He is steadily shortening the distance of his walks. On some beautifully bright mornings or evenings my thoughts go back to times when all three of them ran about playing with each other, after a squirrel, ducks or seagulls. Now, on similar days I meet up with Paul, Hazel, Candy, etc., with their dogs enjoying themselves, whereas when I look back I see Toby plodding along inch by inch, his head down, stopping here and there to sniff the grass or the trunk of a tree. In better days he would be running about under trees, looking up if he'd smelt a squirrel.

It's been a long time since he has looked up a tree or seen the rising or setting of the sun. I now resign myself to the fact that the inevitable day will come, as it did with Gran and Mother; but at least he will not see that dreaded threshold he hated to cross, to be put on the vet's table where he will feel no pain, then once again look up to see a cloud with a gold or silver lining and float through it, once again to be happily united with his mother and grandmother: Cyndy and Becky.

Postscript

It is with profound sadness, beyond words can express, that Toby, in the knowledge of being in the comfort of my arms, parted with a long related companionship just before his fourteenth birthday. It is therefore incumbent on me and the family to dedicate this book to:

Becky

Cyndy

and Toby

– with a change of title to *And Now There Is None.*